THE
CHIMERA
GAMBIT

CHERYL PEÑA

This is a work of fiction. Names, characters, places, and incidents are products of the author's imagination or are used fictitiously and are not to be construed as real. Any resemblance to actual events, locations, organizations, or persons, living or dead, is entirely coincidental.

World Castle Publishing, LLC
Pensacola, Florida
Copyright © 2023 Cheryl Peña
Paperback ISBN: 9798891260085
eBook ISBN: 9798891260092
First Edition World Castle Publishing, LLC, July 17, 2023
http://www.worldcastlepublishing.com
Licensing Notes
Cover: Cheryl Peña
Editor: Karen Fuller

For Michelle Peña Kollin, the coolest little sister I could ever ask for.
Love you, sis.

CHAPTER ONE

"They're firing on us! Why are they firing on us?" the helmsman shouted, feeling betrayed.

"I don't know! Return fire! We don't want to die out here!" Captain Sinclair of the *T-Tauri* shouted back frustratedly. The ship jolted as weapons' fire struck the hull, even as they tried to get into position for an attack.

The Earth ships floated in the black space ahead of them above the small, round platform, suspended blue three-dimensional ghosts in the display hub, as they realized the attackers were their own. Sinclair winced as systems shorted and panels went black before the emergency power clicked on. The dim lights flickered as if they wouldn't hold and then shone brightly like a beacon of hope before the warning sirens sounded for a hull breach.

"Breach!" someone yelled. Sinclair wasn't sure who it was in the gloom.

"Seal that section!" he ordered, hearing a sound like whistling, indicating there might be a tiny breach on the bridge, as well. We're *going down*, he thought. It was inevitable. "Abandon ship and seal the bridge!"

Several faces looked toward him, their pale and frightened expressions reflecting the treachery they were facing from the rest of the fleet. "Sir!" the communications officer protested.

"Abandon ship, goddamnit! Get out of here!"

"No, sir," the helmsman argued, checking his harness to be sure it was secure. "We go with you."

Sinclair didn't want to argue. He didn't want his last moments to be full of anger and fear, but that was what he was facing. Even worse, he was grateful that he wouldn't have to die alone. "Seal the bridge," he ordered again.

They all knew it was a death sentence. Once they sealed it, they couldn't open it again. As the whistling grew louder, they knew it was the only thing they could do to hopefully ensure the survival of the rest of the crew. Securing her harness, communications brought up the ship-wide application and announced the captain's last order.

"Abandon ship, abandon ship," she called.

Operations sealed the doors, the bulkheads clanking loudly into place and irrevocably signaling their fate. Everyone glanced around at the shattered bridge, their last moments playing out differently than any of them had ever expected.

"Return fire," Sinclair ordered again, although the firing had never ceased.

"Pods are away," communications said, hoping they would find their way to safety somehow, even in that inhospitable part of the solar system.

"Why are they doing this?" the helmsman asked uselessly. Who could know? What had they done?

"It's been an honor serving with you," Sinclair managed to say, his breathing becoming labored as the air escaped the room through the breach. "It's been a great honor."

"Yes, sir," the bridge crew agreed, even as they wheezed and gasped for air, immediately before the ship was engulfed in a blinding white light, the hull disintegrating upon impact.

***

"So, what happened to the *T-Tauri*? I thought they were investigating a strange signal out by Neptune," said the Director of Operations for the Outer Division of the International Alliance for Space Exploration, her dark eyes concerned from behind a veil of black hair that she pushed back behind her ear.

"I apologize, Director Weir. We lost contact with them. The rest of the fleet says they never arrived." The man in front of her was her second-in-command, Assistant Director Carlos Nava. He was still young compared to Director Weir. In his early forties, he had a small amount of grey in his short dark hair, but he had already proven his competence and proficiency in his years at the IASE. Natasha Weir trusted him more than she trusted anyone else.

"Did the fleet report anything unusual?" she asked him. They sat in one of the spacious conference rooms rather than in her office, which suited her. She preferred to be in an environment where people didn't expect mementos and photos to be displayed everywhere, revealing precious details about her life that she would prefer to remain private. Instead, the room was spare and surrounded by large, tinted windows. One long black table stretched across the space with several black faux-leather chairs spaced out around it. Director Weir sat at the end of the table with various virtual screens floating in the air near her and resting on the table.

"They only said they engaged a lone B'Noth ship, but it was destroyed. It didn't have a chance to pose a threat, and no transmissions were detected."

Director Weir considered the implications. "The B'Noth don't usually venture this far into our solar system, do they?" she thought aloud.

"No, ma'am," Carlos replied. "Rarely even in the system at all."

She wondered what this meant. Were the B'Noth doing reconnaissance? Spying? Dropping surveillance devices? Mines? "Did the fleet detect anything at all? Any…devices or technology left behind?"

"No, ma'am. Nothing at all."

It was risky, no matter what. The

B'Noth were known to be aggressive, but they usually engaged Terran ships outside the system, sometimes when they were trading with neighboring civilizations or especially if they were traveling alone. What would make them so bold? Approaching Sol, the Terran home system, was like walking across the demilitarized zone alone in a war-torn country and entering the enemy territory unarmed.

"Okay. Thank you. Let me know if we hear from the *T-Tauri,* and keep me apprised of your investigation," Weir responded eventually. She stood, signaling the conversation was over, and Carlos departed with a short bow, indicating acknowledgment, preceding his hurrying out of the room.

Once in the hallway, Carlos wondered what more he could do,

though. He'd requested the reports from the fleet, but so far, there wasn't much they could tell. Until he got the rest of the data, he'd simply be guessing, and that would serve no purpose. What else *could* be done? The fleet had combed the area thoroughly but hadn't found a trace of the missing ship. It was like it had vanished, a mirage that had never truly existed in the first place.

***

Captain James Roden entered the bridge of the *Epirus Nova,* a ragged cargo ship trading outside the Sol system, but now ready to go home. They still had a long journey ahead of them, but he anticipated a raucous celebration that night once he'd told the crew they had completed their run and were heading back to Sol. Some of them may have already guessed, but he hadn't told them officially yet. He sat in the chair in the center of the cramped space. It was on a small dais, but it took only a single step to ascend it. The other stations were close and in a semi-circle around him, but he was used to it. The ship was his, after all. "Ship wide," he said simply.

"Ship wide," the communications officer confirmed.

He looked up at the panel beside him, which had a green light blinking on it, indicating he was transmitting. "*Epirus Nova*, our mission to Varridan is complete. Our next stop is Sol." He could hear cheers echoing even through the thin walls of the ship. "Secure the cargo. Prepare for departure. Roden out."

He smiled, despite his usual stern demeanor. No one expected long speeches from their captain, but he was respected and well-liked among the crew. Perhaps that was because of his proclivity toward brevity and his dislike for those long speeches. But Roden was also known for his generosity and the fact that he never asked more than he was willing to give himself. His own respect for his crew was evident in the way he treated them.

Roden swiveled his chair to face forward again, watching while the preparations were made. The ship would utilize a wormhole to get close to Sol again, but the rest of the journey had to be made more slowly. He couldn't wait to see his home planet again after so much time had passed, however. His crew was his family, of course, but there was nothing like seeing the city of Los Angeles in the twilight, the place he grew up. He still had friends there, so it would be good to see them again after so long. Plus, he was looking forward to real cooked food and fresh air. Already planning his stay, he thought of everyone he would visit and all the sights he would take in before his next cargo run. Home. Earth. Not long now, he told himself.

***

Carlos returned to his spacious office on the top floor, dropping into his padded chair by the wall-sized window like he'd just returned from a funeral. His task was impossible, he thought. Had the B'Noth ship destroyed the *T-Tauri* before it could rendezvous with the rest of the fleet? No. There would have still been some evidence left behind, he reminded himself. What then?

Director Weir's expression haunted him. It was almost as if she'd shown emotion. She wasn't cold by any means, but she was always professional.

Of course, he was in her inner circle, and he knew her better than some others. She didn't feel comfortable around most people to show any vulnerability, but he could tell this time was different. This time, she looked almost troubled. He knew there were bigger issues than just the one missing ship. If the B'Noth were making incursions into Sol, they were all in danger, every citizen of the system. But, even so, there were lives lost under her watch, and she would want to take the blame for it. Perhaps she thought of him as her protégé, but she seemed to watch over him and encourage him to take risks (career-related risks, anyway). He knew his successes at the IASE were mostly due to her.

Not enough time had passed that he would have received the scans and other data from the fleet, so he had some decisions to make. Different scenarios ran through his head, none of them producing answers. What else could he do to find the *T-Tauri*? If they didn't find the ship, there could be fallout as well. And if they did find it, and the B'Noth were responsible for its destruction, they might be at war.

At last, a thought came to him, although he didn't particularly like the idea. He pressed a button and waited for a response. "Yes, Mr. Nava?" came a voice.

"What was the *T-Tauri*'s last known position?" he asked, wishing he already had the data from the fleet.

"Just outside Pluto," came the reply from his assistant.

"Thank you," he said, rising again and rushing out of the room.

***

Carlos had the authority to do it on his own, but he hurried to the conference room where he'd left Director Weir. Unfortunately, it was empty, all signs of previous occupation as absent as the missing ship. Sighing, he checked the timepiece on his wrist, glaring half past noon, and he dejectedly walked back the way he'd come.

"Is anything wrong?" his assistant Leilani asked him, having come up behind him after rushing after him as he'd run down the hall.

He turned and noticed her. "No. Everything is fine. I just wanted to catch the Director before I...never mind. I want you to find me a ship. I'm going to Pluto."

"Are you going personally, sir?" she asked, looking shocked. Nava hated space travel. It made him ill.

He nodded without much enthusiasm. "Yes. We can't spare the fleet if the B'Noth are nearby. So, I have to go."

She acknowledged with a brief nod. "Very good, sir." Then she was gone.

Part of him wished she'd argued a little more forcefully and talked him out of it. The elusive B'Noth may have made a second incursion, he feared, and he didn't want to run into them. No one even really knew what they looked like. Everyone only saw images of their ships before they died. It wasn't a selling point.

He walked back down the hall, debating getting a quick lunch before he decided against it. It would only amplify his nausea when he thought about his upcoming journey. He could already feel his stomach lurching at the very idea of traveling into unknown and dangerous territory. *I must be crazy*, he thought.

***

Natasha Weir sat in the back of the long black floating vehicle that drove her back to her residence on the outskirts of Washington, D.C., ignoring the views out the low windows. The sun was starting to set, and the sky blazed shades of vermillion and marigold as the stars barely began to appear. Instead, her attention was on the virtual tablet she used to read her messages, and she saw a brief note from Carlos Nava. So, he was going to Pluto, she read. It was unexpected, but she knew he would solve the disappearance. That was why she trusted him. His own fears and discomforts were irrelevant. He did what was required of him.

She sent a quick acknowledgement, although he didn't need her approval to do much of anything. It was a courtesy, letting him know that she knew he would be gone and that she would expect his full report upon his return. Although always professional at the IASE, they were as close to being friends as she allowed of work colleagues. They held a mutual respect for each other, but she couldn't allow herself to fear for his life. Maybe Nava had taken the place of her son when he'd gone off to war and didn't come home. Her family was important to her, but then so were her employees at the IASE, although she didn't always treat them with the familiarity they deserved. But she cared for them as much as she could allow herself, even as she knew that losing someone who she cared about hurt more than anything else she'd ever endured. But she didn't have the luxury of taking a moment to think Nava might not return. Not only was it because her own feelings were irrelevant, but answers were imperative, and she would have made the journey herself if she had thought of it first. War might be looming.

***

"Carlos, you can't go!" protested Carlos' wife, Evelyn. She stood in the bedroom doorway with her hands on her hips, daring him to contradict her.

Shaking his head, he had a suitcase open on the bed while he rolled his shirts and pants to keep them from wrinkling during the trip. "Who else can go?" he asked her, a slight challenge in his tone that even he didn't like.

"Oh, I don't know. Just about anyone else!"

She was worried. He couldn't fault her for that, but it was tiresome. "We can't spare any of the others. I'm—"

"Expendable?" she argued.

He sighed angrily. "I didn't say that. I'm not. They don't think I am, either. I'm just saying —"

"That they can do without you. I think that means 'expendable,' doesn't it?" She had changed tactics, no longer using volume to express her dissatisfaction but now switching to open criticisms of the IASE. It was a common strategy that she used, and he was sick of it.

"We don't have expendable people, Evelyn! Why would we send someone who wasn't important when this situation is so damned important?" he yelled.

"What's so important about a missing ship? It's awful, yes. But why is this so urgent? There are people investigating already, aren't there?" She hadn't moved from the doorway as if she were making a barrier of the space between them.

"Yes, of course. But the answer may not be there for them to find. I have to find out what happened because it might involve the B'Noth. We can't have them coming to Sol. We can't." He turned around again, shoving items into the pockets and around the sides of the bag. Although he loved Evelyn, he could feel that they were drifting apart. Arguments were far more frequent than they used to be, and he wished he had more time in a day so that he could make more time for her even while he tried to further his own career.

"Isn't that more of a reason not to go? Or do you have a death wish I wasn't aware of?"

"Stop that. This isn't about me. This is about all of Sol. I can't let fear of the unknown keep me from doing the right thing!" Zipping the sides of the suitcase, he set it on the floor beside him. It barely made a sound on the light-beige carpet.

"I had no idea my husband was so noble!" She'd shouted, but the sarcasm was evident.

He rolled his eyes. "Cut that out! It's insulting. I know you mean it that way, and that's what's so shitty about it." Somehow, the words were coming out without him filtering them, and he felt he couldn't control them if he'd tried. Was this what he was coming to now?

"Oh, so I'm shitty now, am I? I thought we were partners!" she cried.

"I didn't say that. Stop putting words in my mouth." He sat on the end of the mattress and looked at her, heaving breaths in and out like she'd run a marathon.

Her eyes flashed dangerously, and her lips parted as if a retort were coming, but she paused, waving her hand dismissively and spinning around to storm out of the room.

Part of him wanted to go after her to convince her everything would be fine, but he knew he couldn't. She wouldn't see it. She hadn't for years. Although he couldn't understand her bitterness toward the IASE who had provided generously for them for the last several years, he also knew he'd grown distant as he'd moved up the ladder. Maybe it was jealousy on her part. Maybe it was that she was falling out of love with him. That thought hurt him deeply, but he felt powerless to stop it. Everything he'd worked for had been for her, but he was starting to realize that it wasn't what she had wanted. Was it too late now? Was the IASE worth destroying his marriage? Even as he knew this particular trip wasn't about the IASE, even as he felt he had to do something to stop the potential invasion, he knew that it was for everyone, Evelyn included. He wanted her to see that. But was the IASE worth it? What did he want? Did he want to be the next Director? Or was there something else he wanted out of life? Was it too late to try anything else? He wasn't sure the IASE was more important than anything else to him, but was the marriage still capable of being saved? Would she still be there when he returned?

CHAPTER TWO

When Carlos arrived at the port, the stars were fully glimmering in the blackness above him, but there was a flurry of activity around him as everyone scrambled to ready their ships for departure. Many of them were cargo ships, and not all of those had steady schedules. Sometimes they had to leave at odd hours. Leilani had found him a civilian cargo ship heading in the direction he needed to go, and the captain, although not part of the IASE, had agreed to take on a passenger.

Carlos' head swiveled from side to side, gazing around at the busy facility and following the signs to find the correct berth for the shuttle he'd been told to find. There were rows and rows of shuttles, all in neat lines with the berth numbers labeled clearly on lighted signs hanging to the sides of them. Finally, he found 17A, almost hoping there would be a representative or someone there waiting for him. But everyone around him seemed occupied, and no one spared a glance in his direction even as he stood there, obviously out of place with his suitcase trailing along on its wheels behind him. The hatch was open to the aged and scuffed orange and white shuttle, but he couldn't see inside to tell if anyone was there. Nervously, he knocked on the outer fuselage and called out, "Hello?"

A woman with shoulder-length honey blonde hair peered out from the hatch. "Hello?" she responded.

"I'm Carlos Nava. I was told to find 17A, and it would take me to the *Connemara*. I'm the sole passenger."

"Ah, I've been expecting you. I'm glad you got here so quickly. That means we can leave now. Come inside and sit down. I'm Captain Adalynn Adair. The *Connemara* is my ship." She stepped aside, allowing him to enter the cabin while she spoke to someone on her wrist communicator and told them to depart immediately. Then she turned back to Carlos. "Secure your bag. We don't want it to come loose during flight."

There were a few seats in the middle of the miniscule, cramped cabin (which featured the color orange predominantly), but most of them were empty, the rest of the crew already aboard the ship. Carlos found a storage locker mounted on the wall and stowed his bag before sitting next to the captain and securing his harness. He could feel his stomach already rebelling, and they weren't even moving yet.

Adair raised the communicator she was speaking into again, giving orders and announcing their imminent arrival. Carlos could hear the whine indicating the engines were starting up, and his butterflies began to flutter violently. His hands frantically searched the pockets around the seats in front of him until he found a plastic sick bag that he immediately threw up into. With an apologetic expression, he looked at Adair and felt his cheeks flush. She was obviously completely unaffected.

"This part doesn't take long," she

said, noticing his discomfort. "We'll be there shortly."

Well, that wasn't the problem, really, he thought. The entire trip was in space. He wouldn't feel better until they were safely back on land, several weeks from then. However, he didn't voice his concerns, and he only gave a weak smile before he retched again into the bag.

Adair didn't comment on it, and he was grateful that she seemed to know he was monumentally embarrassed. Instead, she swiped her hand across the face of the communicator and watched their progress on a tiny floating screen that appeared above it. Carlos didn't think he could keep his eyes open without embarrassing himself further, so he closed them and tried to breathe slowly, focusing on each intake of air and drawing out the exhale as long as he could. Several uncomfortable minutes passed while he tuned out the captain's voice and everything else going on around him. All he knew was that this was a terrible time for a crisis out by Pluto when he had a crisis brewing at home.

"We're approaching now," Adair informed him at last, and he risked a glance at the display, seeing the representation of the somewhat rectangular *Connemara* looming ever closer. It was a mistake. Quickly, he squeezed his eyes shut tightly and almost frantically tried to do the breathing again. Hearing a loud bang and then a metallic cranking noise, he knew they had docked with the ship. However, his nerves weren't lessened at all. He had weeks of this still to go, he knew.

Adair was standing, and he started to imitate her before he realized his harness was still on. Blushing again, he unhooked the clasps and then retrieved his bag from the locker. "I hate flying," he explained.

She smiled tolerantly but didn't say a word. Leading him away and out the hatch, she turned him over to a young crew member who seemed eager to show him everything there was to see and tell him all about the *Connemara* while the captain left to attend to her duties. Carlos declined a tour, but the young man, who couldn't have been more than seventeen, led him to crew quarters and unlocked one of the doors. Handing Carlos the key, which was a round cylinder with notches on it hung on a lanyard, the man grinned cheerily and departed. Carlos entered the small space, a narrow closet with a cot that was bolted to the wall, a cabinet for storing personal items, and a divider that shielded the toilet and shower from view. He'd be there for at least a month, possibly longer.

He sat exhaustedly on the cot but then remembered that they were going to be leaving orbit as soon as absolutely possible, and he needed to secure himself somehow. Of course, he'd done this before many times for work, even as he'd hated it every time. Looking around the room, he saw that there was a crash chair folded into the wall that he could use if he wanted. There were also belts on the cot to protect him in the event of an incident while he was sleeping. Hopefully, that wouldn't happen while he was aboard. Quickly, he shoved his suitcase into the cabinet and pulled down the seat of the crash chair, securing the harness and wishing he had kept his mouth shut.

***

Captain Roden could already hear the loud chatter, laughter, and off-key singing that indicated the celebrations were already in full swing from far down the corridor. As he entered the mess hall, he saw that some sort of alcohol had already been distributed, as some of the faces were ruddy from the obviously strong brew. A few bloodshot eyes looked guiltily in his direction, but he shook his head and pretended not to notice. He understood. They'd been away from home for almost two years. Most of them had families they were anxious to see. For Roden, this was his life, and his crew were his family.

The room had mostly bare unpainted metal walls and furniture, and it held containers of food and drink that were scattered around the small tables. The tables had benches attached on either side instead of chairs in case the artificial gravity failed. Roden went to a dispenser in the crowded space and poured himself some coffee, preferring to indulge his crew more than himself. Adding a small amount of creamer from the chiller, he turned, then started out of the room.

"Celebrate with us," someone called out.

He laughed lightly but shook his head. "Someone has to fly this thing while you're all getting wasted."

A man sitting at the end of one of the long tables gave him an apologetic look. "Sorry, boss. I can still fly," said the helmsman.

"No. Stay here," Roden replied. "Enjoy yourself. But you don't get to sleep in tomorrow. So, keep that in mind. All of you."

"Yes, sir!" a few voices responded, although there was scattered laughter as well. No one really minded going to work again the next shift as they all wanted to get home as soon as possible anyway.

Roden smiled good-naturedly and walked out, heading back to the bridge, thinking he would be up late anyway. Footsteps rang on the metal deck plating behind him, and he turned, thinking it was the helmsman again, but it wasn't. It was a woman who was relatively new to the crew, and at twenty, she was one of the youngest. She looked shyly at him, but he could guess what she wanted to ask. "Yes, you can drink. I won't tell anyone. But limit yourself to two. That stuff is pretty powerful," he told her, sighing with the feeling he was probably making a mild mistake. He wasn't sure she would even want to drink as many as two glasses. It didn't really taste very good, but it would do the job it was intended to do.

She grinned happily and ran back to the mess hall, practically skipping in excitement. He thought she would regret that decision later, but he shook his head and proceeded down the corridor.

When he sat in his chair on the bridge, he brought up the display hub to make sure there weren't any other ships nearby but saw a couple of B'Noth destroyers at the outer edge of the range of the device. He quickly veered off, hoping they hadn't seen the *Epirus Nova* or that he was too far off to pursue. Nervously, he stared at the display where the B'Noth had dropped off, hoping they wouldn't show up again. For a full thirty minutes, he watched intently, his breathing quickening as he felt a jolt of adrenaline enter his system. Then, he decided to increase speed slightly to put more distance between them, and he sat briefly at the helm to make the corrections before returning to his chair to watch the hub again. Nothing. There was nothing.

Well, that was close, he thought. The B'Noth were everywhere now. It was getting harder and harder to avoid them. Letting his breath out slowly, he leaned back in his chair and tried to puzzle out a solution. But he had none. Instead, he focused on the hub in the center of the room, watching the ship's position as it floated virtually above the device relative to other objects and hoping to avoid a proximity alarm indicating more B'Noth were in the area. Just get home, he thought.

***

Natasha walked the length of the

corridor, appearing almost regal with her suit in a rich, dark burgundy, her sparkling gold jewelry complementing the ensemble. She had a silk blouse of pale gold that shone like a pearl among the shiny metal and expensive wool. At her age, her jet-black hair came from a bottle, and although everyone knew, they couldn't deny the luster and sheen that the color imparted on it. A striking woman, she was also extremely intelligent and managed her job well. She could have retired years earlier, but she rather enjoyed the position and the challenges involved.

However, things were becoming strained. The faces that surrounded her were no longer smiling. People weren't stopping to socialize as before. It signaled that a change was coming, and she worried she would be swept along with it. Was it simply the possibility of war, or was there something else? And did she want to stay to help guide them through, or was she nearing the end of her service? She tried to analyze it like a puzzle, but then she would be late, and that she couldn't do. There was a lot to do before her first meeting of the day, and she didn't want to be unprepared.

Reaching the conference room, she sat down on the far side of the room, taking her seat at the head of the table as usual and bringing up a virtual screen to begin reviewing her messages and the reports she'd been sent. She could conjure a screen anywhere by swiping a sparkling blue data line that ran the length of the table, and the tiny implant in her wrist would verify her identity. The screen would provide a secure link to her own information, but the implant would allow only her to access that data.

A few moments later, she had several screens open, and she compared and contrasted the information, drafting an analysis on another that she had resting in her lap. This was something she was rather skilled at, and she did it quickly, shutting down the additional screens when she no longer needed them.

She had endless meetings scheduled, but the first one was less structured. Leilani arrived and knocked on the door jamb as the door had remained open. "Come in," Natasha requested. "And close the door, if you don't mind."

Leilani did as she was told, choosing a seat near the Director and setting her own screen atop the table. "Is there anything I can do for you?" she asked.

"There isn't, but I appreciate that," Natasha began. "The reason I wanted to speak with you was so that I could check on Carlos. I know you made travel arrangements for him. Have you heard anything further?"

"I haven't heard from him since the ship left the port. The *Connemara*. It's a cargo ship, but they said they sometimes transport passengers. The captain was willing to go to Pluto with Mr. Nava as she said it was on their route. He said he would check in with me periodically."

Natasha nodded, pleased that things were progressing as smoothly as could be expected. "Thank you. Can you please keep me apprised, if you can? It would help him if he didn't have to make reports to both of us."

Leilani agreed. "Yes, ma'am. I'll let him know the next time I hear from him."

"Thank you." Natasha shifted in her chair. "And tell him to be careful." Then, suddenly, she worried that she'd seemed too informal.

Leilani pursed her lips slightly. She liked her boss, and she knew that he and Director Weir were on good terms. "Yes, ma'am."

"I checked the reports this morning. There have been no sightings since the destruction of the *T-Tauri*, but I fear that saying the words will bring bad luck. You can understand that, can't you?" Weir admitted, and Leilani knew what she meant by "sightings" without her specifying.

"Definitely, ma'am. I'm surprised he asked to go. He hates—"

"Space travel. Yes, I know," Natasha finished for her with a slight laugh. "He's doing the right thing, you know?"

Leilani nodded. "Yes, ma'am."

"I would have gone, but he beat me to it. I hope he won't hold it against me," Natasha said wistfully.

"He won't. I'm sure of it."

Weir looked up. "All right. I appreciate you speaking with me. I won't detain you any longer. Thank you for coming."

Leilani stood, bowed slightly, then left the room, leaving the door open again upon her exit.

CHAPTER THREE

Days later, Carlos was bored but terrified at the same time. He tried to keep himself occupied so he wouldn't think about his predicament, hurtling through outer space again. Most of the time, he tried to read or listen to music, but he couldn't ignore the fact that they were a tiny meteor collision away from possible decompression and death. Anything could happen. The hull wasn't thick enough to avert all impacts in the event of a disaster, and he was all too aware of that fact. It was almost as if he could hear the vacuum of space whooshing outside the walls, although he knew that was ridiculous and impossible. But he *sensed* it. It was there whether he could actually hear it or not.

The artificial gravity should have been enough to quell his nausea, as everyone else on the ship was perfectly fine. However, it must have been a mental issue with him because he still felt his stomach doing flips and trying to escape his body through his own mouth. Barely eating, he could only slurp down meal supplements and water. Maybe he was still thinking about home and missing Earth. He realized, however, that he was lonely. All the time. He didn't have a close circle of friends, and Evelyn was really his only company. If she left him, he'd be completely alone. Everything he'd done and sacrificed had led him higher up the ladder, but it had created an emptiness in its wake.

He sat in the mess hall, a small room crammed with various implements and appliances, on a metal bench with his back to the wall, feeling green and like everyone must be judging him. No one had said anything derogatory to his face, but he could see their expressions of pity when they looked at him. It was almost worse than if they'd just insulted him outright.

A plastic pouch of water rested on the table in front of him, and he struggled to keep it down. He knew that if he was vomiting so frequently, he would be dehydrated. It was essential that he consume fluids, and he took deep breaths in between each sip, hoping his stomach would settle and he could try to get something useful done on the trip besides curling on his bunk in the fetal position and wishing he'd stayed on Earth. He'd adjust, of course, but it just took him longer than everyone else.

As soon as he closed his eyes to avoid the sensory conflict of appearing stationary with the opaque walls surrounding him while he also felt the ship's movement, he heard someone else enter the room. He contemplated opening his eyes again, but he didn't think he could manage the effort involved.

"How are you doing?" came Captain Adair's voice. She had a slight lilt as if she were a relatively recent transplant from the British Isles. Ireland? He didn't want to ask.

"I'm sure you can guess," he commented wryly, although without any bitterness. It wasn't her fault he wasn't accustomed to flying.

"My first trip into space, it took me a few days to adjust," she said with some compassion.

He almost laughed. "Well, this isn't my first trip, but I appreciate that."

"Some people aren't cut out for this. Why did you come?" she asked curiously.

How to answer, he thought? "I don't know. It seemed a good idea at the time." He shifted to keep himself upright. The movement seemed to amplify the feeling that they were traveling at great speed, which he knew they were actually doing. "I suppose I want to find out what happened to the missing ship. It could be nothing, but it could be important, too."

"Why you, though? Surely, there was someone else who could come in your place." She sat down across from him, resting her chin on her hand and looking over at him as if he might tell her a fascinating fairy tale instead of the real truth.

"No one else can be spared. The fleet said they encountered a B'Noth ship. If the B'Noth destroyed the *T-Tauri*, we need to know. I didn't think the Director could leave. She might be needed to help avert a war. I didn't think the fleet could spare a ship because they're engaged near Jupiter. I could send my assistant, but that didn't seem fair. I just seemed the only choice."

She partially changed the subject. "How about your family? Were they upset about it?"

"Why would they be?" he asked instead of answering, not sure he felt like expanding on that topic.

Shrugging, she said, "They might

worry that we're heading toward a possible ambush?"

When she worded it that way, he really started to doubt his own reasoning ability. "I don't know that they thought of it that way."

"Why wouldn't they?" She had a packet of coffee that she opened and took a small sip from.

"I don't think…they…*she* just thought I was being reckless because I hate space travel. I'm not sure there was any concern for my safety." Then, he remembered Evelyn's exact words, and there was precisely that.

Adair was holding the packet and staring off, thinking. "It must be nice to be in that position."

"What do you mean?"

"That they're so concerned for your comfort."

He made a face. "Okay, so that wasn't entirely accurate. I guess I just didn't want to think about it. She's afraid the B'Noth will attack us."

"So, an ambush, then?" She smiled crookedly, and he shook his head slightly.

"Yeah, I suppose," he agreed at last.

"Okay. You're fine with that risk, then? That you might not go home to them?"

He felt himself sigh, and he almost felt his stomach contents try to heave themselves onto the table. Carefully, he returned to the slow breathing and took a second to compose his thoughts. "I guess I'm not sure she'll be there when I get back. It wasn't implied, but we've been arguing a lot. I know some of it — or maybe all of it — is my fault. But I'm not sure it would be a great loss to her if I didn't return."

"Then why would she argue with you about it? If she didn't care, wouldn't she just let you leave without saying anything?"

Why was this a subject she was interested in? "You're going to be my marriage counselor? It's fine. We'll deal with it when I go home. If she's not there—" Then what? Was he really okay with Evelyn leaving? Not really, he decided.

"Didn't mean to pry," Adair apologized. "I guess I just find it odd when people with a family head out on dangerous missions like this."

"It's just my wife at present, but yeah." Carlos tried to decide whether he wanted to go back to the privacy of his stateroom or if he felt it was worth it to try to make friends of the crew and stay to socialize. "Do any of you have families?" he asked suddenly.

"Of course. A lot of us do. But cargo isn't always dangerous. Investigating a possible incursion by an enemy is dangerous." She tapped her fingers on the metal tabletop. "I'm just trying to get a measure of you. We don't get a lot of passengers. At least, not often. Usually, it's just us out here. Not many chances to meet people."

He smiled back. "It's fine. I appreciate the offer and the hospitality." Standing cautiously and slowly, he threw the empty water packet into a waste receptacle. "I think I'm going to go lie down. I'm still not feeling well."

"I can give you a patch if you want. I always have them."

He nodded. "Sure. Thank you."

She gave him directions to the

medical quarters. "The doctor will be able to give it to you. Tell him I sent you."

Turning, he left the mess hall and followed her directions, knowing he didn't have time to be sick. He should have asked for help days earlier. Then again, that might be one of his flaws, that he always had to do everything himself, he reflected. Bitterly, he wondered why Evelyn hadn't left him ages ago. He wouldn't have blamed her if she had.

***

Ledett slipped over to Voreth, who stood against a reticulated pillar on the bridge of the B'Noth destroyer *D'Vattash*. The bridge was covered in elaborate patterns, bronze and gold, appropriate for a ship of their importance. Voreth seemed to be surveying the crew's activity from near the pillar, one of several which might have served some sort of function in the wide room, but Ledett was unaware of it. Although Voreth was their captain and First Prime, Ledett knew she was allowed to touch him, and only she. He had told her he was going to promise himself to her. She'd even seen the bracelet, a cuff of jeweled gold that would make her the most powerful woman on B'Noth. But that wasn't her aim at all. She loved him, trusted him.

Their latest mission took them near their deadly archenemy, Earth. It wasn't that they were near the vile planet itself, but they knew there were always patrols in the system, and they could be discovered. The mood on the *D'Vattash* was tense, everyone constantly on guard. She hadn't been alone with Voreth in weeks, which was upsetting to her.

Her hand went up to his cheek, caressing the soft ridges and bumps on his handsome face. "How are you, Beloved?" she asked.

His fingers grasped her wrist and pulled it away. "I am busy now, Ledett."

"You don't have a few moments for me?" she cooed, her fingers again tracing the longer ridge of his face.

"I do not. I cannot let myself lose control. Not ever. I am First Prime, you must remember."

Her hand dropped to her side. "Then, what about me?" she asked, hurt.

He stood still, glaring at her as if she'd struck him. "You must come with me," he ordered, taking her arm and leading her to his quarters. His tone was not playful or endearing. It was cold and indifferent.

Puzzled, she followed along, but she couldn't understand what had happened. He led her down the corridor a short way until they had reached the stateroom she had shared with him for the last year. The room was filled with rich silks and jeweled furniture that befitted his stature as the leader of their home planet. It was usually a place of endless distractions and repose. It didn't feel like that now. He removed her carryall from its drawer, which she'd used many months earlier to bring her belongings to come live with him. Then, he began rummaging through cabinets and drawers, placing her things inside the bag.

"You are no longer required," he said icily. "Pack your things."

Angrily, she took the carryall from him and began folding her clothes, still not understanding what was happening. He stood and watched her while she packed, trying to hurry her.

"I must get back," he argued, his eyes suddenly flicking to the bracelet that he had promised her.

Quickly, she pulled clothes and jewelry and other personal items out of the drawers and cabinets. Then, something dawned on her. "You don't trust me."

His gaze dropped to the floor briefly as if he might have been ashamed. But then, a belligerent expression replaced the look.

"You think I'm going to take the bracelet." She stopped packing, glaring at him. "If the bracelet is all you want, that is all you will have," she declared, taking what few items she'd managed to reclaim and stalking out the door. But what could she do? She couldn't face Voreth any longer. She couldn't face anyone else either, for that matter. Her position was no longer known, no longer at Voreth's side. Anyone could choose to hurt her now, no longer protected by Voreth's position. What place was there for her here if she was vulnerable to retaliation? But for what exactly? Why didn't he trust her? No one else would trust her now, either. They would think she had done something to hurt Voreth or that she had betrayed him.

Would Voreth take any action against her? Would she find her days to be as few as her belongings now that she was no longer in a position of security as Voreth's consort? He no longer trusted her. Why not? What had changed? She would have wept if she wasn't still so confused and terrified. Part of her knew she could be disappeared or killed, but it was hard to imagine after a full year of believing she was safe. Finding herself at the escape pods, she instinctively climbed inside one of them, squeezing through the portal and dragging her bag behind her into the small space. Quickly, she downloaded a packet of data, anything she could find that might protect her, and then she closed the seal and released the clamps, no longer thinking and only reacting. Escape. She had to get away from here. But where could she go in only an escape pod? A shuttle would be noticed, however, and she had to remain hidden. But what could she do in enemy territory?

Her hands shook slightly as she took the controls, speeding away from the *D'Vattash*, forever to be outcast and alone. If she'd stayed, he would have found a way to frame her for some offense, to arrange an accident. Had he found someone else? It didn't matter.

Now she only knew that she was still in danger, and she had nowhere to go. None of the nearby planets supported life. She was in a precarious situation, isolated. But she raced as quickly as she could away from her home and her past, her previous existence now only a memory.

***

The *Epirus Nova* had been traveling for weeks after the celebrations had ended. Now, exhausted and anxious, they had entered the Sol system and were approaching Pluto. "I've got something on the comm. It sounds like a distress signal," communications announced.

Captain Roden watched the display hub as the new object floated into view, a short cylinder with elaborate etchings across the surface in a language he couldn't decipher. His stomach went cold. "It's B'Noth," he whispered.

Several things raced through his mind: destroying the pod, putting as much distance as he could from the thing, and the possibility of even pulling the thing into their hold and rescuing the alien. "Put the audio up," he said while he tried to order his thoughts.

It was in English, which chilled Roden even further. *"Please help me. I'm alone. You're in danger if you don't help me. Please bring me aboard. I need to talk to you."*

The informal nature of the transmission was odd, he thought. Sighing, he came to a decision. "Bring it aboard, but I want guards on that door when we open it," he ordered.

A questioning expression on the officer's face told Roden that communications didn't understand his captain's motivations. "Sir?" the man asked.

"You heard me. We can't take a chance that it isn't a real emergency. Bring that pod on board and post guards. I'll be down there later." Then he let out his breath and cursed. "Of course, this happens when we're almost home," he complained to himself before sending his first officer, Commander Evers, down to meet the alien.

CHAPTER FOUR

When the pod door was opened, the two heavily armed guards stood warily, holding their weapons at the ready. A lone B'Noth woman was inside the cylinder, her hands tightly clutching a shiny grayish overnight bag, which must have held her belongings. She recoiled slightly upon seeing the guards as if she'd never seen humans before and was repulsed. However, she gathered herself and approached the hatch, leaning forward, her arms extending and holding out the bag for them to take as if offering them her worldly possessions in exchange for asylum. Evers took the bag, gesturing for her to keep her hands visible while she climbed out of the pod. Then, she stood, shaking slightly, but she raised her chin and said confidently, "Take me to your captain."

And she said "captain," as if she were aware of their command structure. "You can talk to me," Evers barked.

"You are the captain?" she asked.

"Tell me your story, and if I deem it necessary, I will take you to see him. But you'll talk to me first," Evers said. No one had ever seen a B'Noth before, and he tried to hide his unease at her appearance. She had reddish brown skin covered in rounded ridges and bumps but was obviously female and humanoid. That was the unnerving part.

As she was smaller than they were, she allowed herself to be taken and put into restraints before they walked her toward an empty room with benches and tables in it, the guards standing at attention in the doorway. Evers sat down and gestured to the seat in front of him. She sat, uncomfortable in the strange surroundings, but she looked around her as if it really mattered where she was being held.

"Talk," Evers reiterated sternly, watching her closely for any signs she was hiding a weapon. She was restrained, but it didn't necessarily matter, and no one had wanted to touch her to search her.

Her voice quivering slightly, she began. "My name is Ledett. I am from B'Noth. We have been watching you for decades. That is how I learned your language. But now, we have new technology, technology that allows us to manipulate what you perceive. Our ships are in your system, but not in large numbers. We are waiting for you to destroy yourselves, and you will. We will make sure of it."

Challenging her, Evers shook his head. "Why would you tell me this? You're putting your ships at risk."

Pausing briefly, she clasped her hands in front of her. "I'm telling you because I have nowhere to go. I was outcast. I request asylum. I will tell you anything you wish to know in exchange for my life. You need me, even if you don't know it yet."

"But why would you tell me? You could be lying for all I know." Evers sat back against the chair and crossed his arms over his chest, a barrier.

"We don't have time to debate this.

Your ships are in danger. I will help you, but you need to trust me."

Her dark eyes were almost expressionless and held endless mysteries. He couldn't tell if she meant what she was saying or if she was trying to deceive him. It was impossible to tell what she was thinking or feeling with her alien countenance. What could be her motive? Would she tell him, or was there something else going on? "How can we trust you? You haven't told me anything about yourself."

"I'm defecting. I was outcast. What else do you require?"

"Why were you outcast? That might be important for us to know."

Suddenly, she looked to the table and away from his gaze. "I don't know."

"You have to know. Tell me, or we'll send you back out into space to fend for yourself." He leaned forward slightly, raising his voice, and it frightened her.

Her hands betrayed her anxiety and distress. They wouldn't stop shaking, and she finally put them under the table and out of sight. "I was the consort of the First Prime. He grew tired of me." A reddish droplet of something like liquid splashed onto the tabletop, alarming Evers enough that he thought she needed medical attention.

"Are you injured?" he asked, pointing to the red pool.

Confused, she shook her head in an imitation of a Terran expression in the negative. "I'm fine." Her voice shook.

"What is that?" he asked as another droplet appeared next to the first one, new beads of red moisture appearing on the outside of her skin and glittering in the dim light of the room.

"Nothing. I'm sorry. I'm…weeping. I don't mean to upset you."

"That isn't blood?" he tried to clarify.

"No."

Sitting back again, he tried to regain his composure. "Okay, so you're defecting. How are our ships in danger?"

"We'll make them destroy each other. We can. We've done it before."

He growled. "Stop talking in riddles. What is it that you're doing exactly?"

She wiped away a few of the drops on her face, accidentally smearing the red gelatin-like substance over her hands. "I have information in my bag. I will show it to you. But please take me to your captain. I promise I am telling the truth."

***

"Where is Nava now?" Natasha asked

Leilani. She was in Nava's office this time, standing in front of his assistant and resplendent in a deep green silk dress with her coat draped over it.

"He's almost to Pluto. We should hear from him soon," Leilani replied. "I should have his report in a few minutes."

"Is it okay if I wait with you?" Weir requested, almost shyly, as if she were actually uncomfortable in Leilani's space now that Nava wasn't there.

"Yes, ma'am," said Leilani. Her display showed a chart of the system with Nava's last reported position marked on it. The supposed last known position of the *T-Tauri* was in red, almost exactly where Nava's ship was supposed to be.

They waited silently, both nervously watching the display as if it updated automatically, which it did not. Leilani had turned off the earbud and had her audio ready to play the next transmission when it arrived to the entire room, although she and Weir were the only people present. Hearing static, she turned the volume up and waited. Soon, Carlos Nava's familiar voice came over the speakers.

"We've reached the last place the T-Tauri was known to have been, but there's nothing here at all. It's completely empty. Captain Adair wants to follow the ship's proposed course to Jupiter and see if we can find any wreckage on the way to the rendezvous point. I've sent our scans and position. You should receive it shortly. I'll let you know if anything happens en route. There isn't anything on scanners, but you can't ever tell. I hope everything is fine on Earth. I'll be in touch."

Natasha let her breath out slowly. "Thank goodness for that. Can you please let me know when they reach Jupiter? I have reports to present."

"Yes, ma'am. I'll page you."

"Thank you." Natasha stood from her seat, the dress clinging to her form as she crossed the room and slipped quietly out the door.

***

It had been several weeks, amounting to a month or so, since the destruction of the *T-Tauri*. Rumors were flying among all of the ships in the fleet as everyone tried to understand what had happened to the missing ship. However, as there were few details, no one could really answer them. They speculated and speculated. Most of the captains tried to quash the rumors, but they persisted.

On the *Eye of Horus*, the lead ship in the Terran fleet looking into the IASE ship's disappearance, Tactical Officer

Darzi cursed. "There is a B'Noth fleet massing near Earth!" he called as he stared horrified at his display. The bridge was a wide room with modern glass features in white and chrome, but he turned to face the captain, who sat directly behind him.

Captain Titus Morelli also cursed from his chair at the center of the space, then he turned to Darzi. They were all the way out by Jupiter, still investigating, and he wasn't sure they could reach Earth in time. "What about Delgado's fleet? Why aren't they protecting Earth?" Morelli wanted to know. He wasn't asking anyone in particular, but he sure as hell wanted an answer. Delgado was supposed to be patrolling near the home world to protect it from invasion.

"There's no sign of the other fleet," Darzi told him.

Morelli cursed again. "Full speed.

Signal the fleet. We're going to Earth," he pronounced, frantic.

Darzi sent a message to the other ships, transmitting their new orders and destination. Everyone knew it was hopeless. The planet could already be under attack.

***

Damon Evers reluctantly left Ledett standing in front of the captain, who lay on a couch to one side of his office, where he sometimes spent off-duty hours when he didn't have time to go to his quarters. A blanket was wrapped around him so that Ledett could hardly tell what the captain actually looked like. The Terrans' bland appearance was almost more terrifying than she had imagined. It was uncomfortable being on a ship full of them.

The captain didn't say a word. He

only lay there, enveloped in his shroud, his brown eyes barely showing through a gap in the fabric. "I need to talk to you," she started. There was still nothing. If it was a tactic of some sort, it was working. She was definitely unsettled. "I know you have no reason to believe me, but I am telling the truth. If your ship is destroyed, I will be destroyed with it. I have no reason to lie."

The silence sounded like a deafening boom. It hurt her ears almost more than if he'd screamed at her. He didn't believe her. "I showed the other man the plans for the stealth satellite. We've been watching you. We've learned what we needed to learn to be able to deceive you. We can manipulate your technology to make it appear we are in front of you instead of your own ships. We've done it before. Your fleet is in danger."

The captain lay still, not moving. Had he heard her? She wished he would respond. If he said anything, it would give her a clue as to whether she was convincing him. "I have no desire to return to B'Noth. My lover betrayed me. I'm alone. I want to be useful that you will keep me here. I have no reason to lie nor any motivation to do so either. I want to stay here."

Still nothing. Now, she wasn't sure there was even a man in the blankets at all. Were the eyes even real, or had she imagined them? She stood as confidently as she could manage, standing still and somehow not trembling. "I have told you what you need to know. You must contact your fleet and warn them. They will destroy each other."

Suddenly, there was slight movement from the blanket, and the captain exposed his disturbingly smooth face to look at her. "We will verify what you've told me," he said simply. Then, he knocked on the wall leading to the corridor outside, and Evers returned, leading her away.

"There's no time!" she shouted as she reached the doorway. "The attack is imminent!" But Evers had a firm grip on her arm, and he pulled her into the hallway. She had no choice but to go along, or he would hurt her.

***

Roden had returned to the bridge, with Ledett under guard in crew quarters for the past several days. He sat on the edge of his chair, watching the display hub as it showed an Earth ship in their vicinity. The *Epirus Nova* was approaching Jupiter now, hauling its cargo as quickly as it could across the system, the crew hoping they would be able to stop any disaster from occurring.

There had been chatter from the fleet that a B'Noth armada had surrounded Earth and was preparing for an attack. It was hard to know whom to believe. But could they risk Earth's destruction on the word of a single B'Noth who might be a spy? Roden ground his teeth, thinking intently. "How long has that other ship been there?" he asked finally, returning to the original conundrum.

"A few hours," came the answer.

"Hail them," he said.

"Comm open," replied the officer in communications.

"This is Captain Adalynn Adair of the Connemara,*"* a woman stated calmly. *"How may I assist you?"*

"This is Captain James Roden of the *Epirus Nova*. We picked up a distress signal from an escape pod a few days ago. It held a B'Noth woman. Have you seen any B'Noth ships nearby recently?"

"No, but we're here investigating the disappearance of an Earth ship in the area. It may have been destroyed by the B'Noth, but it's been a few weeks. They've probably gone."

Roden tapped his fingers against his chin. "Have you found anything? Any sign of your ship?"

"Not yet. I can let you know if you're interested."

"Do you require any assistance?" he asked.

"That would be very kind," Adair replied.

"We'll stay in contact," Roden told her. Then, he signaled to cut off the transmission. "What do you think?" he asked Evers, standing next to his chair.

"A B'Noth ship may have been in this area a couple of weeks ago and destroyed an Earth ship. Is that what they think?" Evers asked.

"Yes. Would the B'Noth still be here?"

Evers shook his head slowly. "I don't think so. They're usually in and out. They don't stick around."

"Let's scan for wreckage. If we find anything, it will help us figure out what's going on." Roden then stood and left the room, heading for crew quarters.

***

"Did your ships destroy an Earth ship a few weeks ago?" Roden demanded of Ledett, who curled into a ball in the corner of the cot and tried to disappear.

"No. Your own ships destroyed it. I told you."

"You may have told Evers, but

you didn't tell me. How did you make them destroy it?" He sat down, hoping to appear less threatening, but she didn't move.

"We can make them see what we want them to see. The fleet thought it was a B'Noth ship."

He felt anger welling inside him. "This is the first you've mentioned this. Our fleet destroyed an Earth ship?"

"Yes," she whimpered.

"Where? Here?"

"No. The ship was supposed to rendezvous with the fleet. The fleet destroyed it, thinking it was B'Noth. It's where it was supposed to be all along."

***

"We're here," Adair reported as the *Connemara* approached the rendezvous coordinates near Jupiter. Carlos sat next to her in a folding chair on the bridge, his brown eyes reviewing the data on her display. There was definitely a debris field, but was it the *T-Tauri* or was it B'Noth as the fleet claimed?

Carefully, the ship slowed and began to comb through the wreckage, looking for anything that would identify it. Most of it seemed to be dust, as if the ship had vaporized instead of simply exploding. They sifted through pounds of it, analyzing its density and composition with the *Connemara*'s scanning devices and only being able to tell it was, indeed, a ship. Other than that, it was still a mystery. As they searched around the site, they tried to find any pieces longer than an inch or two in length. However, everything seemed to be nearly microscopic.

They followed the trail of debris toward the coordinates they were given, having contacted the fleet for the information. But as they closed on the site, they still found no clue to the actual identity of the destroyed vessel, only gas and dust.

However, upon arrival, the crew member scanning the debris called out, "I got something!" Adair and Carlos rushed over to see what it was. The virtual display showed a fragment about a foot long that floated and spun in space several yards away from the ship's current position.

"Get a still of that, will you?" Adair requested.

The crew member kept trying, but every image he attempted to capture was either blurry or showed nothing at all. The fragment continued to spin, making it difficult to snap a clear picture of it. Then, finally, a distinct image appeared, and he enlarged it, clarifying the detail as he did so. The name showed clearly: *T-Tauri.*

CHAPTER FIVE

"So, it's our ship," Roden argued after speaking with Adair over the comm. "That doesn't mean our fleet destroyed it."

Evers shrugged. "Can we rendezvous with the *Connemara*? Maybe we can analyze the fragment even further."

Roden considered, but he didn't know that he had any other options. "Captain Adair," he called through the open comm. "We'll be joining you shortly. We may have some information for you."

"Roger that," Adair acknowledged.

"You going to tell her about the defector?" Evers questioned.

Roden nodded. "I think we'll get farther if we're all talking to each other."

"Should we contact the fleet?" Evers asked.

"I think we'll see what this fragment can tell us. I hope that's the right move. But I don't want to trust this B'Noth woman on the sole basis of her word. She might be telling the truth, but she might be trying to deceive us somehow." Nervous, Roden watched the display showing their approach on the *Connemara*.

***

Roden and Adair met on the bridge of the latter captain's ship. Roden had brought

Evers and the defector, whom he had yet to be properly introduced to. Evers held onto Ledett's arm as if he feared she might run away, but he stopped short of keeping her under guard or pulling a weapon on her. However, he had the defector tell her story to the other captain, who was also skeptical.

"Nothing can do that," Adair said.

Ledett appeared distraught. "Maybe you can't, but we can. It's a deception meant to have your ships destroy each other. Then, you will have no defenses. We will be able to attack soon with fewer ships and without any resistance."

"I can't say I like that idea either," Adair agreed, still pacing the bridge. "I don't want to sound paranoid, and I'm not sure they'll believe us even if it's true."

"It's true. You have to try to convince them," Ledett urged her.

"Do we have that fragment you told me about?" Roden asked. "Is it aboard, or is it still floating out in space?"

"It's in the hold." Adair led all of them through the corridors, silently hoping this was some sort of dream. She didn't want the responsibility, the weight of the lives of the fleet crews on her shoulders. What if she was wrong? Well, that would be better than her being right, wouldn't it? Or would it? That would mean the B'Noth were attacking. So, no, neither option was good.

They reached the door, and Adair opened it, leading them inside where the fragment was under a forcefield on a table while a couple of people in environmental suits were inside the field running tests of some sort on it.

"Is that really necessary?" Roden asked, puzzled.

"I don't want to chance anything at all, Captain. This is standard for us when doing tests on unknown substances. It's not exactly something we do often, but we prefer to use caution."

Roden approached the outer edge of the forcefield and watched the scans. "Is there anything you can tell us about that?"

One of the suited people looked at him and nodded. "Yes. It's definitely one of our ships. It has to be the *T-Tauri*. The composition is a match. Trace elements show it was…." The man paused, gathering himself. "It appears it was friendly fire that destroyed the ship, however. The weapon's signature is Terran."

***

Roden, Adair, Evers, and Ledett rushed back to the bridge, running as fast as they could through the semi-crowded corridors. Upon reaching the bridge, Adair sat in her chair and ordered the communications officer to contact the fleet.

"We can try, captain, but they're too far away for a clear signal," the man said.

"Do what you can," Adair confirmed.

Carlos looked confused. "What's going on?" he asked from his chair. He'd remained behind when everyone else headed to the hold.

"Friendly fire," Adair told him. "Friendly fire destroyed the *T-Tauri*."

"So, she's telling the truth?" Carlos tried to clarify.

"It appears so."

He quickly rose and went to the communications officer to send his report to Weir and Leilani. Although he hadn't composed it yet, he hurriedly scrambled to put a few words together and to transmit them. However, he knew it would be a while before it was received. It wasn't clear how much time they really had to save the fleet. Would his efforts mean anything at all, or would the fleets end up destroying each other?

"We need to get back to Earth," Carlos insisted. "If we can't reach the fleet and convince them…." He left the rest unsaid.

"Captain, we're heading for Earth. Are you staying here?" Adair asked Roden.

"No, we'll follow you," Roden replied. An officer signaled Adair that he would lead them back to the shuttle bay, and Roden, Evers, and Ledett practically sprinted after him, sensing the urgency. Please let us not be too late, Roden thought.

***

A few weeks later, the Terran fleet closed on Earth in a haphazard manner, no longer caring that they had stragglers and a few ships out of formation. Their home world was under attack. Morelli could see the B'Noth ships on the display hub, floating red in three-dimensions around the orb that indicated the planet Earth. They had not yet opened fire, to Morelli's great relief and puzzlement, but he knew he had to act fast.

The *Eye of Horus*, Morelli's destroyer, launched its fighters and advanced on the lead B'Noth ship, firing weapons and signaling the other ships in the fleet to begin their assault. As each ship arrived, it began to follow the *Eye of Horus'* lead, attacking the B'Noth before they could mount a defense.

Suddenly, Darzi called out, "We're receiving a transmission from the lead B'Noth ship!"

Morelli, surprised, said, "Put it on the screen."

A male B'Noth appeared in front of them on the virtual screen in the front of the room, barking out something unintelligible as the translation matrix couldn't keep up with him. It sounded like furious gibberish, and Morelli only wished he could tell if the man was offering to surrender. It didn't sound like a surrender, however. It sounded like a threat.

"Cut it off," he said finally, not being able to make any sense of it anyway.

"What do we do?" asked the

communications officer.

"Resume firing. We cannot allow them to take Earth," Morelli ordered irritably.

"They're signaling again," Darzi informed them from tactical.

Morelli said nothing. He only stared at the display showing the ship positions and the battle taking place before them.

***

"We're still too far away," Roden complained as they were still not able to tell what was happening near Earth, although they had pushed hard to get that far. They were closing fast but couldn't see the fleet on the hub. "Can we get a signal through?"

"We can hear them, but they don't appear to hear us," replied communications.

Roden groaned. This was the worst-case scenario he was afraid of. "Can we safely increase speed?"

"I wouldn't recommend it, captain," said the helmsman.

"Well, there may not be a fleet left to protect if we don't get there soon!" Roden pressed.

The helmsman increased speed.

"They say they've engaged the B'Noth," communications informed them.

"Tell them it's not the B'Noth!" Roden shouted.

Several seconds passed. "They're not responding."

"Are they receiving?" Roden asked.

"They appear to be, but they just don't answer."

Roden cursed under his breath. "What's going on?" he asked Ledett. "Why can't they hear us?"

"They can hear you. They just think you're speaking B'Noth," she responded.

"What can we do?" he asked her urgently. "We can't just sit here and let them destroy each other."

"The stealth satellite. I gave the plans to you. If you destroy the satellite, they will see clearly."

"Where is the satellite?" Roden asked, frustrated by the apparent lack of useful information. It was like pulling teeth to get to the nuggets Ledett had finally given them.

She shook her head. "I don't know its current position. I wasn't involved in that. But I downloaded the data before I left my ship. You can use that to track it."

"We don't have time for this!" he shouted again.

Ledett recoiled. "I'm sorry. I wish I knew more."

He turned to Evers. "Do you have the plans? Maybe we can get Captain Adair's help with it."

"Yes, sir. I'll get on it now," Evers replied, coming to attention and then departing.

Roden rubbed his eyes. Now or never.

***

Adair received the transmission from the *Epirus Nova*. It was from Evers, plans for a stealth satellite that he said the B'Noth had developed. Captain Roden was requesting their help in finding it. Evers had said it was responsible for the fleets attacking each other.

"Can you analyze this?" she asked Carlos, who was still sitting beside her as a high-ranking official guest.

He nodded, determined, then swiped the data line in the arm of the chair to bring up a screen. Then he pulled the data over from her display, his hand grasping it in the air and then flicking it until it appeared on his screen. The satellite had a low power signature and would be nearly impossible to find, he thought. Reading the data, he tried to find a weakness, something that would help them to track it. But, after hurriedly analyzing the plans, it didn't appear to even emit any radiation or reflect light. Feeling pressured, he knew they didn't have much time.

"Can I see the current scans of Earth?" he requested.

Adair nodded absent-mindedly, but she swiped something on her display, and he was suddenly able to see the data. He sifted through it in a rush, trying to be methodical about it, but he definitely felt pressured. They were running out of time. He had to find it and find it soon. Nothing in the scans stood out to him, but he thought he knew what to look for. It wasn't so much that he was searching for something out of place, but something that wasn't there at all. He looked for a gap in the background radiation around the planet, something that looked like an anomaly. The stealth technology definitely made the satellite difficult to find, but he knew they had to save the fleet from the current deception and Earth from a future attack. Hurry, he told himself. Hurry.

***

Morelli shouted, "Fire, fire, fire!" as the B'Noth began to fight back. The battle was taking a toll on the fleet, as several ships had exploded into fragments due to the enemy fire, but they'd destroyed a few of the opposition as well. The lead B'Noth ship repeatedly transmitted its pointless message as no one could understand a word, and the ship's systems couldn't, either. The *Eye of Horus* was taking heavy damage, but they couldn't let Earth fall. Many of the fighters had been taken out, but they swarmed like bees around the enemy armada, who had unleashed theirs as well. Morelli tried to protect his own fighters by targeting the small B'Noth fighters and striking them with his own weapons. But they were all more maneuverable and much too fast for his ship. He sent a few torpedoes toward the lead destroyer, but even that seemed pointless. The fighters took out the torpedoes before they could hit their intended targets.

But their distraction was working. The B'Noth had not fired any weapons on the planet. All their attention was focused on the fleet, who were assailing them furiously. Morelli winced as a panel shorted in front of him and went black. An alarm was sounding somewhere in the background, but he ignored it, his eyes on the display hub as ships winked out in front of him. When the overhead lights went out, he waited momentarily before the emergency systems kicked on, then he shouted, "Return fire!" as if his crew needed any motivation. They fired without hesitation. The hub display sputtered briefly but then shone brightly again. "Target that lead ship!" he ordered.

"They're signaling again," Darzi said uselessly.

"Ignore it. It's pointless," Morelli responded. "Just fire on that ship!"

***

"I've got it!" Carlos yelled excitedly, hoping that was true.

Adair glanced over, then saw the apparent black hole, a circular absence of data floating in orbit around Earth. Carlos touched it on the screen, but it was obvious something was there once he'd sifted through all of the data and pointed it out. The anomaly had to be the satellite. It was like something had blotted out the light behind it, even as it floated amid the other space debris around Earth.

The captain sent the data to the helm, and the dark sphere appeared on the display hub in front of the room. "Helm, get us there now!"

"Yes, captain!" came the acknowledgement, and the *Connemara* changed direction. It was no longer heading for the fleet but for Earth. All they knew was that the satellite was manipulating their perceptions, and it had to be destroyed one way or another before they destroyed each other.

They watched the display intently, watching the fleet movements now that they were close enough to see them, the firefight playing out before them in miniature on the hub, ships turning into bright flashes of light before they winked out and disappeared. Many ships were already gone. The B'Noth were probably watching happily as their plan played out perfectly.

***

Suddenly, a new B'Noth ship showed up on the display, and Morelli watched it closely. It wasn't engaging the fleet, but its trajectory marked it as heading for the planet. "Pursue that ship. It's going to launch weapons on Earth!" he fretted. His own ship was barely holding together, but he knew his fleet was Earth's only line of defense. Delgado and his own fleet were nowhere to be found. Perhaps they'd already been destroyed.

Morelli was tired. He wanted it to be over, but they had no choice but to fight. They raced away from the battle, desperately trying to stop the attack. The enemy ship was way ahead of them, but they accelerated to close the distance, only to see another destroyer as it rushed to intercept them. A message was being transmitted, but it was more B'Noth gibberish, so he turned it off.

"There are two of them!" Darzi exclaimed, watching the new ships join the battle.

But the two ships seemed determined to reach another goal. They weren't going after the fleet. The only alternative was that they intended to do something to Earth, although that seemed a strange moment to do so with their armada under attack. Whatever they were planning, Morelli knew it would mean wide-scale destruction on the planet, and he had no intention of letting them get away with it.

He called for a few fighters to join him, ordering the rest of the fleet to continue engaging the B'Noth armada. Six fighters zoomed across his field of vision, rapidly closing the gap between them and the new ships. "Fire!" he ordered again. The fighters flew around the second ship, their weapons tearing holes in the hull as they attacked.

CHAPTER SIX

Roden felt sadness overtake him as his ship took damage. He only knew he had to intercept the fleet and protect the *Connemara*, who had managed to overtake him and were heading for what he hoped was the satellite. Of course, he didn't have the data they had, but he had heard through the comm that they were heading for the coordinates of a suspicious object. The *Epirus Nova* raced in front of the *Eye of Horus* as it pursued the *Connemara*, but that only made it easier for them to attack it.

Hull breach warnings sounded, and Roden called for the sections to be sealed. "Stay away from the damaged sections!" he called out.

Some of the displays had gone dark at the first barrage of weapons fire, and there were technicians working furiously to repair them. However, it seemed hopeless. More weapons' strikes caused the ship to shudder, and then more warnings went off.

"We're venting atmosphere! Life support is offline!" someone shouted.

"Send a distress signal!" Roden ordered, hoping the *Eye of Horus* would call off their attack. They were helpless, and he didn't want his crew to die. *Please*, he thought. *Help us.*

***

The *Connemara* reached the coordinates

and nearly crashed into the satellite before they found it. It was nearly invisible. "Destroy it," Adair ordered.

"The *Epirus Nova* is hailing us. It's a distress call," said communications.

"Our best chance to help them is to destroy that satellite. Fire!"

A single torpedo sped away, but a Terran fighter intercepted it, and it exploded uselessly only meters away from the satellite. "No!" Carlos protested.

"Fire again! Destroy it! Now!" Adair ordered again, seeing several Terran fighters approaching her field of vision on the hub and readying an attack.

They fired another torpedo and another. Communications repeatedly called into the comm that they were an Earth ship, but none of the fighters answered them. They were almost on top of the satellite, and Adair considered simply ramming it, but there was no guarantee the thing would sustain enough damage to stop functioning. She watched as each of their torpedoes were destroyed, then they had no choice but to fire the weaker plasma weapons. "Fire!"

A fighter crossed the beam and exploded into fragments and dust in front of them, but the beam continued past the debris. It burned a hole into the satellite, streaming hot metal at the surface of it until it suddenly broke apart, fracturing like glass, the power source rupturing and causing the interior gases to luminesce and combust. A ball of hot gas exploded outward, and it struck the hull of the *Connemara*, causing systems to short and the lights to go out, but thankfully, there was no major damage. Strangely, as soon as the thing was destroyed, Adair felt hope.

***

"Please, cease fire!" cried Captain Delgado, appearing suddenly on Morelli's screen and looking beaten and bruised, the bridge of his previously state-of-the-art ship in tatters behind him.

Morelli, confused and actually frightened, called, "Cease fire!" as he saw the Earth ships scattered on the display, the B'Noth nowhere in sight. "Cease fire!" he ordered.

Darzi looked to where the two B'Noth ships had headed for Earth, but two cargo ships had replaced them. "What just happened?" the man asked.

"I don't know," Morelli admitted.

"We're receiving a distress call. It's the *Epirus Nova*, a cargo ship."

Morelli heard someone comment, "Where did that come from?" but he ignored the statement.

"Respond. Tell them we're on the way," Morelli said. He sighed deeply, not understanding the turn of events, and he wondered if this were somehow a deception. Were they still B'Noth? Hopefully, someone had an answer.

They approached the cargo ship warily, still not quite trusting that it was what it appeared to be when only moments ago, there had been a B'Noth destroyer there. Docking with the ship, however, they hurried to provide medical aid to anyone who needed it, sending teams into the damaged ship to rescue the injured crew and assist in the evacuation. They hurried, seeing the engines' temperature rising and fearing they had little time. When all of the crew were accounted for, including a lone B'Noth woman who the obviously

Terran captain insisted be brought along, they released the ship and sped away, heading toward a rendezvous with the *Connemara*.

Captain Roden and the B'Noth woman were brought to the *Eye of Horus'* bridge while the rest of the rescued crew waited in the hold due to the lack of available space. When they reached the battered bridge, they were astounded that the ship was still in one piece. Fragments of the equipment came out of nowhere in the darkness as they approached the captain. "What happened out there?" Morelli demanded when they reached him.

"It's hard to explain," Roden said. "But this woman here saved us." He told Morelli about finding the escape pod and everything that had happened since. "We came as fast as we could to warn you."

Morelli looked around his bridge, some of the systems still offline from the attack and thought of all the ships that had been lost, all of them apparently on the same side, unbeknownst to him. He sat down, putting his head in his hands and taking a few deep breaths.

"It wasn't your fault," Roden told him, reading his actions as a sign of remorse. "You were deceived. The satellite has been destroyed. We have the plans as well, so we can mount a defense against it if this ever happens again."

Finally, Morelli sat up straight, wiping his eyes and staring ahead as if traumatized. It would take years to get over what happened, he knew. It didn't matter that there had been technological interference. He'd destroyed several Earth ships. *He* had. Then, he glanced at Ledett, who shyly looked at the floor and twiddled with her thumbs. "Thank you," Morelli said honestly, glad the attack had been stopped before there had been even more casualties.

Then, they were led away, allowed to join the others in the hold as the *Connemara* arrived.

***

Several hours later, Carlos pulled up into the driveway of his house and turned off the engine. The lights were out, but it was late. He picked up his bag from the seat next to him and then carried it with him to the front door. Anxiously, he unlocked the front door and slipped inside, flipping the switch and seeing the mostly empty rooms around him. She's gone, he thought. She's gone.

Nearly collapsing on the sofa, he set his bag down, defeatedly looking around him. There were a few pieces of furniture still there, but most of the décor was obviously packed and taken away. Only the sofa and a small cot in one corner indicated that she had thought of him at all. The rooms looked bare without their photos on the walls and the small mementos from vacations they'd been on together. It was as if she'd left only the shell of his life behind. With only the job left, he wasn't sure he was happy with how his life was turning out. He was truly alone. He had thought it was possible that she might leave, but seeing it for certain took the wind out of him. Although he was now seen as one of the heroes who had helped save the fleet, he couldn't save the one thing that mattered the most to him. Perhaps she knew it was over when she didn't continue the argument. She'd just walked away from him, unlike during previous disagreements. He guessed he should have known when he didn't try to stop her from walking away and when he didn't chase her down to convince her he was right. But he still felt like a failure. Love didn't understand such things. He only knew it hurt that she was gone.

***

The next morning, Carlos joined Natasha Weir in one of the conference rooms, per their usual routine. It seemed very normal, but it was not a normal day. He sat down across from her, where she had her usual screens open before her.

Closing them one by one, she gazed at him and smiled warmly. "How are you doing, Carlos?" she asked. It was unusual, even for her, to call him by his first name. Yes, today was different.

How did one answer a question like that, though, he wondered? He'd been up half the night trying to figure that out. Although he thought he had found a solution, he was far from certain. "I'm fine," he lied. "The *Epirus Nova* is being repaired, and the crew are well. The B'Noth defector is safe and is being introduced to some people who will help her. She'll be given a home, and she promises to provide intelligence to Earth in exchange for asylum. Morelli of the *Eye of Horus* will have a tough time for a while, though. But I think he'll survive it all. How are you?"

She sighed. "Not fine," she said honestly. "A lot has happened. We're going to be facing a lot of fallout because of the fleet. I don't want all of it to fall on the fleet commanders, so I'll probably take most of the blame myself."

"I'm sorry," he told her.

She shifted in her seat, looking

older than she usually did. "You're the hero of the moment. I don't want to take you down with me," she continued. "I think it might be time that I retire."

"What will you do?" he asked.

"Nothing. I think I just want to spend more time with my family. I miss them. I've worked long enough and given enough years to the IASE. I don't think they'd fault me for my dedication. But I think it's finally time."

"You will be missed," he admitted.

"I want you to take my position," Natasha told him. "You would make a great Director."

Smiling, he shook his head. "No. I appreciate the offer. But I have something else in mind. I'm resigning, too."

Shocked, she looked down at the table and then back up at him. "I wish you luck in whatever you do."

"Thank you, Natasha," he said, using her given name for the first time as they were both now considered civilians and no longer part of the IASE. "I'll always consider you a friend."

She wiped away a single tear that had managed to find its way onto her cheek. "And I you."

***

A few days had passed, taken up with media interviews and visits with family and friends, old and new. Captain Adalynn Adair waited in the port nearly a week later, standing next to the shuttle in berth 17A, where she'd first met Carlos Nava. Although she'd missed home, she was ready to start the next run, ready to get back to her normal job. She didn't have to wait long. Soon, Carlos appeared at the end of the walkway, and she closed the distance to greet him.

"Are you sure this is what you want to do?" she asked, still surprised after receiving the first message from him a few nights earlier.

He nodded. "I'm as sure as I'll ever be. It's time for a change. I want to do this." His bag rolled behind him as before, but now he was a civilian, and he would have to work for his room and board. The thought was terrifying and exhilarating, as he wasn't sure what to expect on a cargo run, but he definitely felt ready to find out.

She laughed lightly. "You don't know how rare that is. Most of us debate leaving every day."

"Really?" he asked, completely incredulous.

"Of course not," she answered. "I was joking."

He shook his head but followed

her as she led him to the shuttle and opened the hatch. "You always hated space travel. Why now?" she pried.

Thinking, he wasn't even sure he had a clear answer. "I like what you do. I like the idea that you're extremely important, but you don't have to make the same sort of life-or-death decisions every day like I did as part of the IASE. I like that you're close to each other and you have friends with you everywhere you go. That's what I want from here on out. I don't want to be alone anymore."

She grinned at him. "I think you have a different view of us than we do. But we're glad to have you on board."

"I hope I didn't offend you," he worried.

"No. Just the opposite. But you'll see. It's not easy by any means. You'll work hard. But it's rewarding. And yes, it's important."

He climbed through the hatch and set his bag into the same storage locker he'd used before, then sat down next to Adalynn and secured his harness.

"I brought some extra sick bags just for you," she teased.

He laughed, then took a few deep breaths. "I think the last trip did it for me. I was okay once we started investigating and everything. It just helped me to focus on something else for a while. I think I'll be okay."

"You declined the tour the last time. If you're going to work with us, I think it's time you learn the layout then. What do you think?" She had a slight smile that he found enigmatic and intoxicating. He couldn't help feeling trepidation and intrigue in equal measure.

"I agree. Show me everything.

Show me the stars."

"You got it," she acknowledged, smiling. "Let's go."

END

ACKNOWLEDGMENTS

This was a fun novella to write, but it didn't come together immediately. It started out as a short story, but it's evolved into this slightly longer form through the help and support of several people.

First, I have to thank my first beta reader and good friend, Hermione Lee, who helped to develop this story from a quick adventure story into something a little more profound. I would also like to thank Heather Dixon for enduring several rounds of cover suggestions and helping me to narrow down my own choices. I'm terribly indecisive! My father, Alfredo Peña, always supports me in everything I choose to do. Thank you so much for going on this journey with me! It means more than you know. Also, my mother, Charlotte Peña, keeps me sane when I get stressed (which is a lot), and I couldn't do this without her support. Thanks for learning (probably) more than you ever wanted to know about publishing! Inge Pratt started this whole endeavor by suggesting I publish my first novella, *The House of Wynne Lift*, and although it is very different from *The Chimera Gambit*, I hope it is as fun to read as it was to write. I can't forget to thank Inge for her enthusiasm for my writing and for encouraging me to reach beyond my comfort zone. Also, thank you to my readers! You make this all worthwhile, and I appreciate your enthusiasm for my books, even when I keep you up past bedtime. Last, but as always, *certainly not least*, I have to thank Karen Fuller who always creates something amazing out of my clumsy words) and everyone at World Castle Publishing for making these stories of mine into stunningly beautiful books. Thank you so much!

ABOUT THE AUTHOR

Cheryl Peña was born in San Antonio, Texas, to multiracial parents and grew up with an interest in art and literature. Before she was able to read, she was writing books in one way or another. By age ten, she had reached college-level language skills and won first place in the National Language Arts Olympiad when she was eleven years old. She graduated with an honors BFA in photography and worked as a professional photographer for a couple of years before eventually settling in the legal field. Upon the death of her twin sister in 2014, she decided to write professionally in her sister's honor. She is the author of the thriller novella *The House of Wynne Lift*, as well as the science-fiction *Descent of the Vile* duology. *The Chimera Gambit* is her first science-fiction novella.